The After-Christmas Tree

Story by Linda Wagner Tyler

Pictures by Susan Davis

PUFFIN BOOKS

PUFFIN BOOKS
Published by the Penguin Group
Penguin Books USA Inc., 375 Hudson Street, New York, New York 10014, U.S.A.
Penguin Books Ltd, 27 Wrights Lane, London W8 5TZ, England
Penguin Books Australia Ltd, Ringwood, Victoria, Australia
Penguin Books Canada Ltd, 10 Alcorn Avenue, Toronto, Ontario, Canada M4V 3B2
Penguin Books (N.Z.) Ltd, 182–190 Wairau Road, Auckland 10, New Zealand

Penguin Books Ltd, Registered Offices: Harmondsworth, Middlesex, England

First published in the United States of America by Viking Penguin, a division of Penguin Books USA Inc., 1990
Published in Puffin Books, 1992

10 9 8 7 6 5 4 3 2 1

LIBRARY OF CONGRESS CATALOGING-IN-PUBLICATION DATA
Tyler, Linda Wagner.
    The after-Christmas tree / by Linda Wagner Tyler: illustrated by Susan Davis   p. cm.
    Summary: Family members take their Christmas tree into the backyard and decorate it
    with edible trimmings for the wild birds and animals.
    ISBN 0-14-054191-8
    [1. Christmas trees—Fiction. 2. Christmas–Fiction.] I. Davis,
Susan, 1948–   ill. II. Title.
[PZ7.T94Af 1992]   [E]—dc20   92-8616

Printed in the United States of America
Set in Bookman Light

For my Mom and Dad,
thanks for my wonderful childhood years.
—L.W.T.

For Sally, my twin, with love.
—S.D.

It was New Year's Day.
It was time to take down the Christmas tree.

I feel sad when Christmas is over.

We had fun making cards
and presents and
baking cookies.

Mom and Dad came to see our Christmas pageant.

We had a caroling party.

And we found the perfect Christmas tree. It was so tall we had to make extra paper chains to fill it up.

MISTER B.'s
TREES

"Why does such a great season have to end
so soon?" I asked Mom.
Mom said, "I have an idea to make it last longer.
Let's have a winter party."

THE
TYLERS

✤ Please
come to our
After Christmas Party
Meet at the pond
on Saturday at 2 p.m.
Bring your ice skates.

We made invitations and sent them to our friends.

We spent the afternoon taking the decorations
and lights off our tree.

On Saturday we met at the pond.

The ice was like glass.

When it was time to go home we gave everyone a bag and asked them to collect pinecones on the walk back.

Dad made popcorn and Mom said, "We are going to
decorate our old Christmas tree with treats for the birds
and wild animals so they will have enough food
for the long winter ahead."

We gathered around the table and
covered the pinecones with peanut butter

and rolled them in birdseed.
We strung popcorn and berries.

Dad set the tree up in our yard.

We tied the pinecones to the branches with red ribbons.

Mom gave us nuts to spread around the base
of the tree.

When we were finished, our old tree didn't look so sad anymore. Then we went inside.

Mom and Dad passed out the hot chocolate
while we watched the party outside.

There were birds all over the Christmas tree and the squirrels were stuffing their cheeks. Mom said, "Our Christmas tree is enjoying its second season of giving."